MR. NOSEY

by Roger Hargreaves

DEAN

Mr Nosey liked to know about everything that was going on.

He was always poking his nose into other people's business.

Mr Nosey was the sort of a person who, if he came upon a locked door, couldn't resist looking through the keyhole to see why the door had been locked.

Mr Nosey was the sort of a person who, if he found an unopened letter addressed to somebody else, would simply have to open it to find out what was inside.

Mr Nosey was the sort of a person who, if he was sitting reading his paper on a train, would much rather read the paper of the person sitting next to him.

Naturally, as you might well imagine, Mr Nosey was not very popular.

People did not like the way in which Mr Nosey would peek and pry into their affairs.

They did not like it at all, but did that stop Mr Nosey peeking and prying?

It did not!

Mr Nosey lived in a funny, tall, thin house in a place called Tiddletown.

The people of Tiddletown decided that Mr Nosey was becoming much too nosey, and so they held a meeting to discuss what to do about him.

"We must find some way of stopping him being so nosey," said old Mr Chips the town carpenter.

"That's right!" said Mrs Washer, who ran the Tiddletown laundry. "He needs to be taught a lesson."

"If only we could think of a way to stop him poking his nose into everything," said Mr Brush the painter.

And then a small smile spread over his face.

"Listen," he said, now grinning. "I have a plan!"

All his friends gathered round to listen to his plan.

The following morning, Mr Nosey was out walking along Tiddletown High Street when he heard somebody whistling behind one of the closed doors.

"I wonder what's going on here?" he thought to himself and, tiptoeing up to the door, he quietly opened it and peeped in.

SPLASH! went a very wet paintbrush right on the end of Mr Nosey's nose, covering it with bright red paint.

"Oh dear. I AM sorry!" said Mr Brush, who was painting the inside of the door.

Poor Mr Nosey had to go straight home to try and remove the red paint, which was very difficult and rather painful.

Mr Brush chuckled to himself.

The Plan had begun.

The following day, Mr Nosey was walking past the laundry when he heard somebody laughing on the other side of the wall.

"I wonder what's going on here?" he thought to himself and, standing on tiptoe, he looked over the wall.

SNAP! went a clothes peg right on the end of Mr Nosey's nose.

"Oh dear. I AM sorry!" said Mrs Washer, who was hanging up clothes on a washing line on the other side of the wall.

Poor Mr Nosey removed the clothes peg, and went off down the street feeling extremely sorry for himself and for his poor red nose.

Mrs Washer chuckled to herself.

The Plan was working.

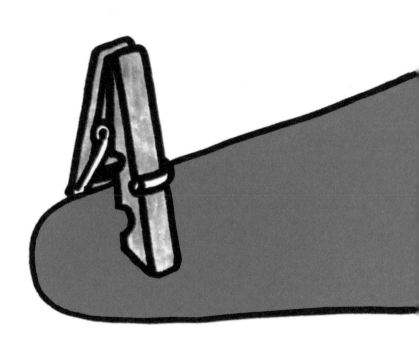

The next day, Mr Nosey was going past a fence when he heard hammering.

"I wonder what's going on here?" he thought to himself and, creeping very quietly to the end of the fence, he peeped round.

BANG! went a hammer right on the end of Mr Nosey's nose.

"Oh dear. I AM sorry!" said old Mr Chips, who was nailing up a loose plank in the fence.

Poor Mr Nosey had to go home immediately and bandage his poor red sore nose.

Mr Chips grinned a broad grin.

The Plan was working very well indeed.

The following day, Mr Nosey was walking in the woods when he heard somebody sawing wood.

"I wonder what's going on here?" he thought to himself, and he crept up behind a tree.

He was just about to peer out from behind the tree when it suddenly occurred to him that if he did, something very nasty might happen to his nose.

And so he went on his way without being nosey.

Behind the tree, with a saw raised in his hand, stood Mr Herd the farmer.

When he saw that Mr Nosey had gone on his way without being nosey, he laughed and laughed and laughed.

The Plan had worked.

Mr Herd hurried into Tiddletown to tell everybody.

The Plan really had worked because after that Mr Nosey stopped being nosey and soon became very good friends with everybody in Tiddletown.

And that is the end of the story, except to say that if you are ever tempted to be as nosey as Mr Nosey used to be, you'd better expect one thing.

A sore nose!